The Baseball Bat

Written by Ski Michaels
Illustrated by George Guz

Troll Associates

Library of Congress Cataloging in Publication Data

The baseball bat.

Summary: Bart Bat wants to join his animal friends
on their baseball team, even though he usually sleeps
during daylight hours when they are playing.
    [1. Baseball—Fiction. 2. Bats—Fiction.
3. Animals—Fiction]   I. Guzzi, George, ill.
II. Title.
PZ7.P3656Bas   1986   [E]   85-14065
ISBN 0-8167-0596-8 (lib. bdg.)
ISBN 0-8167-0597-6 (pbk.)

10   9   8   7   6   5   4   3   2   1

The Baseball Bat

"Hooray for baseball!"
yelled Bart.
Bart Bat liked baseball. He liked
baseball a lot. Bart liked to play
baseball. He wanted to be on a
baseball team.

Babe Bear was on a baseball team. Babe Bear was a good hitter. Babe could hit the ball far.

Tom Cat was on a baseball
team. Tom was a good pitcher.
He could pitch fast.

Sandy Rabbit was on a baseball
team. She was the team captain.
Sandy Rabbit was a good
catcher.

"I can pitch," said Bart Bat.
"I can hit and catch. I want to
play baseball. I want to be on a
team."

"*Whooo* said that?" asked Ollie
Owl, perched up in a tree.
"I did," said Bart.
"You cannot be on a baseball
team," said Ollie.
Bart looked at the owl.
"Why not?" he asked.

"You are a bat," said Ollie. "Bats go out at night. At night it is dark. You can fly in the dark. But you cannot play baseball in the dark."

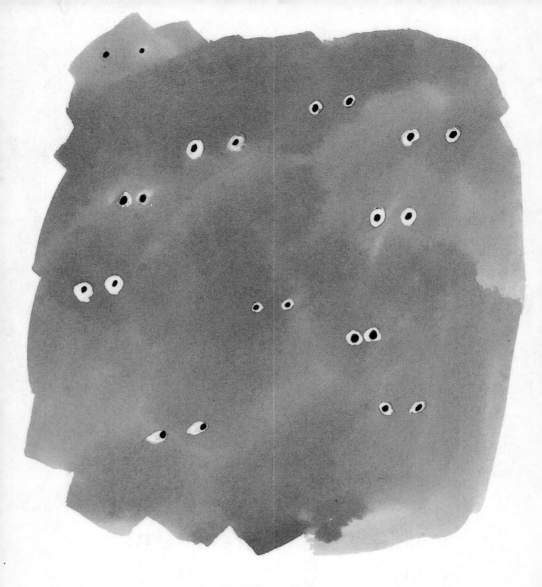

Poor Bart! The owl was right.
Baseball is played in the light.
At night it is too dark to play.

"What can I do?" cried Bart. "I sleep when it is light. Bats like to sleep all day. But I want to play baseball."

13

Ollie Owl looked at Bart.
"You cannot play and sleep,
too," he said.
Then away he flew. He flew into
the dark woods.

Bart looked into the woods. He
saw fireflies. The fireflies were
lighting up the woods with their
special little lights.

"I will not sleep in the light,"
said Bart. "I will play baseball
when it is light. I want to play.
Hooray for baseball!"

Away flew Bart Bat. He flew
into the woods, right past the
fireflies. Away he went.

The next day Bart did not sleep.
He did not sleep when it was
light. Bart went to see Sandy
Rabbit.

"I am a baseball bat," said Bart.
"I want to be on your team."

"You can try out for the team,"
said Sandy.

"Hooray!" yelled Bart.

Bart and Sandy went to the
baseball field. All the players
were there. Babe Bear was at the
field. Babe was hitting baseballs.
What a good hitter he was!

Tom Cat was at the mound.
Tom was pitching baseballs.
What a fast pitcher he was!

"Go out in the field," said
Sandy. "Let me see you catch
some baseballs."
"Hooray!" yelled Bart.
Out he went.

Bart wanted to play baseball.
But bats fly all night. They sleep
in the light. Bart had not slept
all day. When you do not sleep,
you get tired.

Tired? Bart was very tired. He
was tired from flying. He was
tired from being up all night.
Bart was too tired to play.

What happened to Bart? Bart went to sleep, right in the middle of the baseball field. A baseball field is not a good place to sleep.

WHIZ! Tom Cat pitched a baseball. BONK! Babe Bear hit it. He hit it far.

Sandy caught the ball.
"Catch," Sandy yelled.
She threw the ball to Bart.
WHIZ! BONK! Bart woke up!
"Ouch!" he cried. "What hit me?"

The players went up to Bart.
"A baseball hit you," said Babe
Bear.
"Are you okay?" asked Tom Cat.

Bart rubbed his head.
"I am okay," he said. "I want to
play baseball."

"Let me see you hit," said Sandy
Rabbit. "Go up to home base.
Tom Cat will pitch to you."

Bart Bat went up to home base.
He wanted to hit. He wanted to
hit the ball far. Did he?

No! Bart was too tired to hit.
He was too tired to play baseball.
The little bat went to sleep. He
went to sleep at home base.

Tom pitched. WHIZ!
"Strike!" yelled Babe Bear.
WHIZ! WHIZ!
"Strike! Strike! The batter is out," cried Babe Bear.

Poor Bart! He wanted to play baseball. But he was too tired.

Bart went home. He slept all
day. At night he woke up. He
went out in the dark.

"Did you play baseball?" said
Ollie Owl.
"No," said Bart. "I was too
sleepy to play. But I still like
baseball."
"I like baseball, too," said the
owl. "I like baseball a lot. But
owls wake up at night. At night
it is too dark for baseball."

37

"If we had lights we could play baseball," said Bart.
He looked into the woods. The little fireflies were flying about. There were lots of little lights in the woods.

"Fireflies!" cried Bart. "Lots of fireflies give off lots of light. We will have a baseball team. It will be a special team. Do not go away, Ollie."

Away flew the bat. Off he went
into the dark woods.

"I will not go away," said Ollie.
"I want to play baseball. I want
to be on your special team."

Bart flew up to a firefly.
"Do you like baseball?" he said.
"Would you like to be on a
baseball team?"

"I like baseball," said the firefly.
"All the fireflies in the woods like
baseball. We like to play baseball.
We like to watch baseball."

"Hooray!" yelled Bart. "We will have a baseball team. Ollie Owl will be on the team. I will be on the team. And lots of fireflies will be on the team."

And what a team they had! Bart
Bat's special team played games
at night. Baseball can be played
at night with lots of light. And a
team of fireflies gives off a lot of
light.

Bart's team played lots of games. They played Sandy Rabbit's team. What a good game it was!

WHIZ! Tom Cat pitched for
Sandy's team. WHIZ! Ollie
pitched for his team. BONK!
Babe Bear hit baseballs.
HOORAY! The fireflies made
good catches in the field.

And Bart Bat? Bart was not sleepy at night. He pitched, caught, and hit. What a good player he was. All the players cheered for him.

"Three cheers!" they cried. "Three cheers for Bart the Baseball Bat!"

WE LOVE BART

WE LOVE BART

YEA BART

BART IS THE BEST